Noisy Neesha

Written by Lynne Rickards

Illustrated by Sarah Jennings

Collins

Mr Hare was reading the paper. All of a sudden, he heard …

“Hmm,” he said to himself. “What is that noise?”

Mr Hare put down his paper. The noise was coming from the flat above. He went quickly upstairs to see what it was.

tap
tap
tap

"I am trying to read, Mrs Elephant. What is that noise?"

"I'm sorry, Mr Hare," said Mrs Elephant.
"My daughter Neesha and her friend Lulu
love to jump and stomp to music."

The next day, Mr Hare was sitting in the garden.

Mr Hare looked up. What was that terrible racket?

"Sorry, Mr Hare," called Mrs Elephant.
"Neesha is playing her trumpet."

On Friday, Mr Hare was making a toy plane. He was assembling the wing and fixing the final part when ...

CRASH!

"What is going on up here?" asked Mr Hare. He was getting annoyed. Now his fur was all gooey with glue.

“Sorry, Mr Hare,” said Mrs Elephant.
“Neesha dropped the cake tin and the trolley fell over.”

On Saturday, Mr Hare was practising his clarinet.

It wasn't easy to focus.

Bang! Whizz! Pop!

BANG!

"Sorry, Mr Hare," said Neesha. "We were blowing up balloons."

Later, Mr Hare heard an even louder noise. It made the room shake and dust fell down the chimney.

Then he heard his bell.

Ding, dong!

“We are having a party,” said Neesha. “Will you come, Mr Hare?”

“Please?” said all her friends. “The party is for you!”

"What a lovely surprise!" said Mr Hare.

"Thank you, Neesha. You are so kind."

It was a very noisy party. And this time, Mr Hare didn't mind a bit. He was having a wonderful time!

"Thank you, noisy Neesha!"

honk

honk!

POP!

Mr Hare and Noisy Neesha

After reading

Letters and Sounds: Phase 5

Word count: 306

Focus phonemes: /igh/ y, /ai/ a, /ee/ e, ey, y, /oo/ u, /l/ le, /f/ ph, /w/ wh, /v/ ve, /z/ se

Common exception words: of, to, the, are, said, Mr, Mrs, friend, were

Curriculum links: PSHE

National Curriculum learning objectives: Spoken language: articulate and justify answers, arguments and opinions; Reading / Word reading: apply phonic knowledge and skills as the route to decode words, read accurately by blending sounds in unfamiliar words containing GPCs that have been taught, read other words of more than one syllable that contain taught GPCs, read aloud accurately books that are consistent with their developing phonic knowledge; Reading / Comprehension: understand both the books they can already read accurately and fluently ... by: making inferences on the basis of what is being said and done

Developing fluency

- Your child may enjoy hearing you read the book. Model reading with lots of expression.
- You could read the main text on each page and ask your child to read the sound effect words.

Phonic practice

- Look at pages 12–13. Ask your child:
  - Can you find any words that end with the letters **ey**? (*trolley, gooey*)
  - What sound does **ey** make in these words? (*/ee/*)
- Practise sounding out the words and then blending the sounds together.
  t/r/o/ll/ey trolley
  g/oo/ey gooey
- Now explore different ways to write the /ee/ phoneme.
- Look at page 18. Ask your child:
  - Can you find a word that ends with the /ee/ phoneme? (*party*)
  - How is the /ee/ phoneme spelt in this word? (*y*)
- Look at page 16. Ask your child:
  - Can you find a word that contains the /ee/ phoneme? (*even*)
  - How is the /ee/ phoneme spelt in this word? (*e-e*)